PUFFIN

Harry and the Dinosaurs
The Snow Smashers!

Ian Whybrow is a bestselling author of over a hundred books who is proud to have been listed as one of the top ten most-read writers in UK libraries. Among his most popular characters are the hugely successful Harry and the Bucketful of Dinosaurs, the barking mad Sniff and the much-loved Little Wolf. Ian lives in London and Herefordshire.

www.harryandthedinosaurs.co.uk

Look out for more adventures with
Harry and the Dinosaurs:

ROAR TO THE RESCUE!

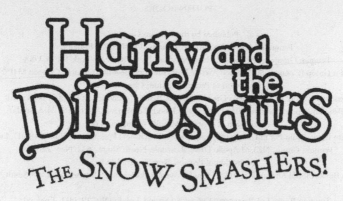

Harry and the Dinosaurs

THE SNOW SMASHERS!

Ian Whybrow

Illustrated by Pedro Penizzotto

PUFFIN

PUFFIN BOOKS

Published by the Penguin Group
Penguin Books Ltd, 80 Strand, London WC2R 0RL, England
Penguin Group (USA) Inc., 375 Hudson Street, New York, New York 10014, USA
Penguin Group (Canada), 90 Eglinton Avenue East, Suite 700, Toronto, Ontario, Canada M4P 2Y3
(a division of Pearson Penguin Canada Inc.)
Penguin Ireland, 25 St Stephen's Green, Dublin 2, Ireland (a division of Penguin Books Ltd)
Penguin Group (Australia), 250 Camberwell Road, Camberwell, Victoria 3124, Australia
(a division of Pearson Australia Group Pty Ltd)
Penguin Books India Pvt Ltd, 11 Community Centre, Panchsheel Park, New Delhi – 110 017, India
Penguin Group (NZ), 67 Apollo Drive, Rosedale, North Shore 0632, New Zealand
(a division of Pearson New Zealand Ltd)
Penguin Books (South Africa) (Pty) Ltd, 24 Sturdee Avenue, Rosebank, Johannesburg 2196, South Africa

Penguin Books Ltd, Registered Offices: 80 Strand, London WC2R 0RL, England

puffinbooks.com

First published 2011
004

Text copyright © Ian Whybrow, 2011
Cover illustration copyright © Adrian Reynolds, 2011
Text illustrations copyright © Puffin Books, 2011
Character concept copyright © Ian Whybrow and Adrian Reynolds, 2011
All rights reserved

The moral right of the author and illustrators has been asserted

Set in Bembo Infant
Printed in Great Britain by Clays Ltd, St Ives plc

British Library Cataloguing in Publication Data
A CIP catalogue record for this book is available from the British Library

ISBN: 978-0-141-33279-6

www.greenpenguin.co.uk

MIX
Paper from
responsible sources
FSC® C018179

Penguin Books is committed to a sustainable
future for our business, our readers and our planet.
This book is made from Forest Stewardship
Council™ certified paper.

ALWAYS LEARNING   **PEARSON**

For the Campbell children:

Anna, Thomas, Laura and Sophie

Chapter 1

Harry had no idea that he was in danger.

His boots
were too busy
making prints on
the crisp blank
page
of the
bright white
snow-filled
garden.

He loved the way the snow crunched when his boots sank deep. He loved the creak it made when he stepped forward. They said on TV it was the best snowfall for a hundred years. And look at it now! At least another ten centimetres had fallen overnight – with more to come.

Harry hadn't been to school for three days. Neither had the rest of his friends in the GOGOs (the Grand Order of the Great Oak), Jack, Charlie and Siri.

Could it get any better? He turned to admire his footwork.

WHUMP!

Out of the blue, two snowballs hit him.
One knocked his woolly hat off. The other
exploded right on his neck.

'Yikes!' Harry shrieked.

'Shot, Boris!' yelled Sam as they ran off,
cackling with laughter.

Harry turned to see the grinning faces of his sister and her smug new boyfriend, Boris. *What a sneaky trick!* he thought. And how annoying that they had made him squeal like a piglet!

'I never miss!' boasted Boris as he and Sam ducked into the house.

Now there was no way Harry could get them back. He stared at them as they made faces at him through the kitchen door. 'You wait!' he yelled.

'Ha-ha!' they replied, acting as if they were as young as Harry.

I need back-up! Harry thought to himself. Thankfully he knew just where he could call on some. He ripped off one of his gloves and thrust his hand into the pocket of his

jeans. He found the little collection of shiny
cards that had appeared on his key-ring
one day ... Help was at hand!

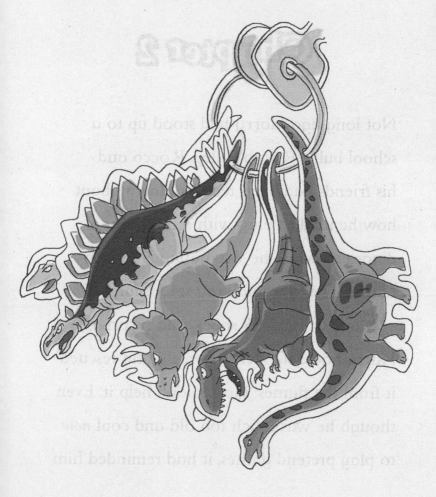

Chapter 2

Not long ago Harry had stood up to a
school bully, Rocco Wiley. Rocco and
his friends had been teasing Harry about
how he used to play with a bucketful of
dinosaurs when he was younger. Rocco
had set fire to a small toy spinosaurus.

Much to Rocco's shock and surprise,
Harry had defended it fiercely and rescued
it from the flames. He couldn't help it. Even
though he was much too old and cool *now*
to play pretend games, it had reminded him

of the years of pleasure his dinosaur friends
used to bring him.

But that night a huge *living* spinosaurus
had turned up in his bedroom. A twelve-
metre-long reptile with the smell of meat
on its breath and a snout like some weird

crocodile. In a voice like air escaping from a burst tyre the spinosaurus had told Harry he was a B.U.D.

– a *Back-Up Dinosaur*. He explained that the dinosaurs that had meant so much to Harry as a little kid had never really gone away. Harry thought he had grown out of them, but the dinosaurs knew that deep down he still believed in them. They were just waiting for him to give them a sign.

They got their sign when Harry took the burnt and wounded spinosaurus from the playground, wiped it clean and hid it

in an empty box of
plasters at home.
That simple act of
kindness meant
that dinosaurs still
mattered to him.
They wanted
somehow to return his loyalty.

They understood that now Harry was
older he couldn't very well carry a bucket
around with him, so the spinosaurus had
told him that if he was in need of help,
he should check in his pocket for his key-
ring. There he would find a collection of
small, flat 'plasticated' Back-Up Dinosaurs,
waiting to be brought to life. To activate a
B.U.D. all he had to do was rub it with his

finger or thumb, nose-to-tail, and the right dinosaur would appear for the job. They would turn up full-size, though Harry could make them smaller if he needed to. And they would always be invisible unless he instructed them to show themselves.

That same night, before he'd gone to sleep, he'd checked and the B.U.D. keyring was right there in his pocket, just as Spinosaurus had promised.

Now, in the snow-filled garden, Harry's fingers and thumb spread the cards. Eagerly he began to feel each one for signs of activation. A B.U.D. that was warm to the touch was ready to help.

But there was no heat at all. The cards were just cold pieces of plastic.

Harry sighed, but then quickly cheered up. 'What am I worrying about? Getting hit by a couple of snowballs isn't serious. I don't need dinosaurs to help me with that. But I know who can – Jack, Charlie and Siri! The GOGOs will give me all the back-up I need!'

Chapter 3

It was great in the woods. At first the GOGOs did nothing except just stand together under the Great Oak and quietly marvel. Everything felt new and special. They watched for a long time as the trees filled up with feathers of snow. Then they felt a sudden need to run about. But after a while that got them worried in case their tracks led strangers to their secret meeting place. Luckily Siri had one of his brainwaves.

'Order! Order!' he said with a grin. 'I see that we are wearing almost the same kind of boots.'

'Only yours are bigger than my dad's!' laughed Charlie, tucking her wild black curls under the ear-flaps of her fake-fur Russian hat.

'I shall rise above rude remarks,'
said Siri. 'Here is what we do: we
go well away from the Great Oak
and trample the snow around lots
of trees. That way even Sherlock
Holmes would have trouble
guessing which tree is our hideout.'

'Good one!' everybody yelled.

The four GOGOs dashed off in every
direction, having the time of their lives in
the enchanted woods, making tracks and
snow-angels among the unspoilt drifts.

Five minutes later, Harry was giving Siri a leg-up on the rope ladder and Jack and Charlie were hoisting him from above. Very soon the gang was snug and warm in the secret chamber deep in the trunk of the ancient oak tree. For many years kids had squeezed together here and smoothed the wooden walls with their bodies. Now the

GOGOs sat, knees tucked up to their chests, facing one another over the glow from a bicycle lamp.

'I wish this snow would last forever,' said Jack, breaking the silence. He didn't talk much, but now he was speaking for them all. 'No school! Wicked!'

'It's all right for you,' grumbled Siri. 'My

parents keep giving me loads of extra maths and English.'

'Never mind, we're here now,' said Harry. 'Let's enjoy it while we can. And I've got an idea. My sneaky sister and her annoying boyfriend, Boris, attacked me this morning. How about you all help me get them back in a snowball fight?'

Everybody started shouting at once, but Charlie managed to make herself heard. 'I've got a better idea,' she said, pulling Siri's woolly hat down over his eyes to quieten him, and getting Jack in a playful headlock. 'We enter the village snow-sculpture competition.'

'But we've already *made* snowmen, dozens of them,' complained Siri.

'Oh, come on,' said Harry. 'It's a great idea. We might never get this much snow again! And when have we ever had snow that *lasts*? I remember once I could only scrape together enough to make a teeny little snowman on a plate.'

'Exactly my point,' said Charlie. 'And anyway, the competition's not about snow*men*. It's about sculptures.'

'Where's it happening?' asked Jack.

'On the green by the village hall,' said Charlie. 'The first prize is a four-man racing toboggan!'

Siri and Harry looked at each other excitedly. 'Then what are we waiting for?' they yelled.

'Yeah, but Charlie,' teased Jack, 'if it's a four-*man* toboggan, where are *you* going to sit?'

Before she could give him what for, Jack shot up through the sacking door above

them like a squirrel. He clambered down
the Greak Oak and scampered away into
the woods, the rest of the GOGOs soon
chasing after him.

Chapter 4

When the GOGOs arrived at the village
green, they could see that they didn't have
much of a chance of winning first prize.
There were loads of sculptures already,
but one was really outstanding – a pirate
ship! It was the work of Tom Powell, the
local handyman and carpenter. As well as
the ship, there was a castle and a tractor
that were really good. But the prize of the
toboggan was too good to miss, so they
wanted to give it their best shot.

After collecting entry forms and being
given a space to build their sculptures, the
GOGOs got to work. Everyone agreed
that Charlie was the most artistic of the

group. She got started
straight away on a
polar bear. Siri and
Jack decided to
work together on
an igloo. Harry
helped them at
first, but they all kept getting in each other's
way and knocking bits of wall over. So he
left his friends to it. He thought he would
have a go at an alligator instead.

Without a photograph to guide him,
Harry struggled to get the shape right.

He worked patiently for fifteen minutes. Charlie took a break from her work and came over to see what he was doing. 'It certainly is big,' she said. 'What is it, a triceratops?'

'No, it's not!' snapped Harry. But when he stood back, he could see what she meant.

It wasn't much good, but it certainly looked more like a triceratops than an alligator. It had the three horns and the bony shield behind its neck. How did *that* happen? Annoyed with himself, he trod all over his work and spoilt it.

'Well, what was it meant to be?' asked Charlie.

'Wait till I've finished and you'll see,' said Harry and started again.

Charlie went back to her polar bear as Harry had another go. This time, he stretched out the shape more, trying to get the tail and the jaws right.

After a while it was Siri and Jack's turn to come over and inspect his work.

'Ace!' said Siri. 'I might have guessed

you'd do one of those!'

'Yeah. That is some apatosaurus!' said
Jack, impressed.

'What are you talking about?' snapped
Harry again. But they were right. This was
no alligator. The long neck and whip-like

tail of the creature definitely made it an apatosaurus. It was as if the snow had a mind of its own! *Something very strange was going on.*

But Harry had no time to think about it. Charlie had nearly finished her polar bear and Jack and Siri needed help making snow-blocks for their igloo. They were at the tricky stage where the middle of the domed roof needed to be filled in. How could they make it stay up?

'Jack and I will stand in the middle,' said Siri bossily. 'Harry will pass Jack blocks as rapidly as possible. Jack will put them in place and I will hold everything up.'

It's never going to work, Harry thought. Still, he couldn't come up with a better way, so

he started to lift the first snow-block ready
to pass it over to Jack.

Suddenly there was a mighty roar, so
loud it made Harry jump and drop the
block on Jack's boots.

Everyone ducked and covered their heads
to protect themselves.

Chapter 5

Almost immediately they relaxed. The
GOGOs had all heard that sound plenty
of times before in the village, especially
Harry. Phew! It was only Wedge, Sam's ex-
boyfriend, driving by in his shiny black 4x4
half-truck. They turned to admire the truck,
its great wheels churning up packed snow
as it skidded to a halt. Wow!

Wedge opened the door and leapt to
the ground. In spite of the cold, he wasn't
wearing a coat – just his checked shirt with

the sleeves rolled up and a pair of ragged
jeans. Everything about the eighteen-year-
old was big – his grin, his scruffy hair, his
strong arms, his hands, even his country
accent.

'I see you're going for the toboggan, then!' he said to Harry, admiringly. 'Did you do that polar bear an' all?'

'Charlie did,' said Harry.

'Cool,' Wedge said with a grin. 'One of these has got to be the winner! Unless . . . Cor, this old igloo is gonna be a cracker, too, once you've got the roof on!'

Good old Wedge, thought Harry. *He always says the right thing. Sam must be mad to be going out with that snob Boris instead. Just because Boris is rich and drives a sports car!*

'Hey, maybe this'll help.' Wedge fetched a large plastic container with a spray attachment from the cab of his truck. 'This is what you need to keep the roof nice and solid,' he told the GOGOs. 'It'll be a bit like welding, only using quick-freezin' water instead . . .'

Talk of welding made Harry remember a disaster from when he was younger. Mum hadn't noticed his scooter lying behind her car in the driveway and had reversed over it. Harry was heartbroken, but Wedge had told him not to worry, and took the wrecked scooter off to his workshop. By the end of the afternoon, he had straightened it out and welded the handlebars back on, good as new!

Wedge gave Jack and Siri a quick demonstration of ice-welding, but couldn't stay. 'I need to get back home to help Dad rescue some sheep stuck up on the hill. Talking of which . . . Did you hear about the road up to Huntingdon getting blocked? The whole village is trapped!'

'How many people live up there?' called Charlie, pausing from her work on the polar bear's paws.

'Well, there's a dozen houses at least,' sighed Wedge. 'And there's quite a lot of old folks up there an' all. Let's hope they've got plenty of fuel and food until the emergency services can get to them, eh?'

'Maybe they can work together and dig themselves out,' said Siri.

'Nah, mate!' said Wedge, shaking his head. 'It's at least a mile up the lane to Huntingdon from the bottom road, and it's sunk right deep in places. Diggin' out would take weeks. Anyway, I'd better be off!'

By the time the sound of the truck's big engine faded away, two of the igloo's roof-blocks were firmly in place. 'Nearly ready for moving into!' chuckled Siri.

Not long after that, Jack was crawling out of the entrance giving a thumbs-up. 'It's wicked in here!' he smiled. 'Really snug. No wonder Inuits like igloos!'

The GOGOs completed their entry forms
and dropped them off with Mrs Jenkins
inside the hall. Then they set off at a run to
find other ways to enjoy the snow, just in
case it did all disappear!

Chapter 6

Harry was woken very early next morning by the sound of cows bellowing. He flicked on his light, knelt on his bed and opened the curtains. Long icicles hung like sparkling spears from the gutter just above his window.

Glancing down towards the lane, he saw Mr Oakley and his friend Mr Standing driving cattle up towards Mr Oakley's farm. Harry threw open the window, shouting, 'Mr Oakley! Do you need a hand?'

Mr Oakley looked up and waved to Harry in the window. 'You're all right, Harry! We're just shifting this lot up to the barn,' he called.

'They broke through a hedge and got down to the water-meadows and on to my lake,' explained Mr Standing. 'Skidding

about, they were!' As a cow went astray, he tucked a firm hand under her chin and steered her back into the lane. 'Good to see you've got your lights on, boy,' he added. 'I saw on the telly that they've had so much ice in some places it's brought down the electricity lines.'

Harry suddenly remembered the people in the village on the hill. 'Does that mean the power's off in Huntingdon?'

'Very likely,' said Mr Oakley.

'Well, who's going to rescue the villagers?' asked Harry.

'Helicopter, maybe,' said Mr Oakley. 'If it's not too busy with other emergencies.'

There must be something somebody *can do for them*, Harry thought. At that moment Sam burst into his room.

'Close that window, Harry!' she hissed. 'You're letting all the heat out of the house!'

Harry ignored her. Mr Standing was calling out again. 'You want to get down later on and take a look at my lake if you fancy a bit of skating. I tell you, if it's thick enough to stand this herd on, it's safe enough for you lot.'

'Fantastic! Thanks,' said Harry, thrilled. He waved and pulled his window closed as the herd lumbered slowly on up the lane. Behind him, his sister stamped and made noises. It was tempting to say something rude about moody cows. But this was not the right moment. Instead, Harry said brightly, 'Can I borrow your skates, Sam? Pleeeease! I've got permission to skate on Mr Standing's lake.'

'No way!' she snapped.

'Why? Are you going to use them?'

'No, Boris is coming round with a golf DVD. We're watching it together. He was going to take me to the golf course, but it's closed because of the snow.'

'There you are, then! You won't need your skates if you're staying in.'

'I told you no! I'm not having you messing them up.' She slammed the door behind her as she stomped off.

Harry's heart sank. Sam was always annoying, but he was sure she'd got worse since she went all soppy about Boris. Now he was turning her into a golf-freak! Sam said Boris was 'mature', but Harry thought he was nothing but a pain.

Sam and Boris were always taking over

the living-room sofa. That stopped Harry watching the only TV in the house that didn't make your eyes go funny. Nobody else got a look-in with those two watching recordings of golf matches. He still couldn't believe that Boris's idea of fun was writing down in a notebook every single shot each golfer played and which club they used. How boring!

Harry missed Wedge. Wedge was nice to him and really knew how to have a laugh. It made Harry smile even now when he remembered him doing his party trick. Sam hadn't seemed to realize how lucky she'd been to have a boyfriend who could play 'God Save the Queen' on the hose of the vacuum cleaner.

If only they could get back together, Harry thought, before heading off to phone the GOGOs and tell them about Mr Standing's ice rink.

Chapter 7

It was great to be out of the house and away from Sam and Boring Boris. Harry dashed off as fast as he could to Mr Standing's farm. He had arranged to meet the GOGOs there for a 'non-sledge' race before they got on the ice.

They'd all agreed that you could count anything as a non-sledge except a purpose-built sledge or a toboggan. So Charlie

unscrewed the wheels from her famous
dragon skateboard and turned up with a

dragon *snow*board
under her arm. Jack
brought along a
plastic tea-tray with
handles on two
sides.

Siri arrived lugging an enormous

cardboard box. It was
the packaging from a
fridge-freezer that
his mum and dad
had bought in the
sales. 'Fridge-freezer.
Cool. Get it?' He
grinned.

Charlie rolled her eyes, then she turned to Harry. 'Where's your non-sledge, Harry?' she demanded.

Harry smiled. 'In my pocket. Ta-dah!'

 With a flourish like a magician, he whipped out a shiny black, heavy-duty bin-liner. 'Take your marks here for the Downhill Challenge!'

The starting line for the race was at the top of a track that led down a steep pasture.

'Listen up, racers!' called Harry. 'We go through that gap where that five-bar gate is open. OK? After that, we follow the track through the trees. Then we get on to a really, *really* steep slope down to the edge of the lake, so be careful. First one to the lake is the winner!'

Jack was a bit worried that Siri would have no chance in his box and wanted to give him a head start.

'You are a gentleman and I thank you,' smiled Siri. 'But I will be perfectly fine. I have thought a great deal about the design of this machine.'

He laid the box on its side, dived head first into it, then his head popped out of a hole in the other end. He thrust his arms out of big slits in the sides and waved them about. 'My engines and also my brakes!' he beamed. 'The bottom is polished with

beeswax. I am confident that I shall go like
a rocket. Ready when you are!'

Jack was small enough to sit with his
knees up to his chest and his heels on the
edge of his tea-tray. Charlie was poised on
her snowboard. Harry tucked himself into
his bin-liner as if it were a sleeping bag. He

pulled it right up to his chin and flipped himself on to his back.

'3 ... 2 ... 1 ... LIFT OFF!' Harry yelled. He arched his back like a loopy caterpillar and smacked his heels down into the snow to get himself moving.

Jack was away first, hanging on to the handles of his tray for dear life. Braking and steering were out of the question, but he didn't mind. He just leaned his body this way and that. By the time he arrived among the trees, he was just ahead of Charlie. She'd hit a root and fallen off her dragon-board at the gate. But she'd got quickly back in the race and was now speeding along faster than any of the others.

Harry wasn't far behind. *Ooh-ah-ooh!* He

felt every lump and
bump of the track
through the thin
plastic of the bin-liner,
but he didn't care. It just
added to the thrill!

Siri had a terrible start.
His arms weren't long
enough to give him much of
a push-off and his legs were
trapped in the box. Still, he
had the advantage of being the
heaviest racer, which helped when
he hit the steep slope beyond the trees.

By then Charlie had already arrived
at the edge of the lake. 'Yesssss!' she
yelled. But as she bent down to lift her

board out of the way, Jack crash-landed
into her and sent her flying. Harry slithered
into the pair of them. Siri, however, was
still coming down the hill at them like a
runaway train.

'GET OUT OF THE WAY!' he yelled,
but it was too late.

KERPOW!

WAHOOO! FLUMP!

FLUMP!

FLUMP!

The four of them piled into the snow in a
wiggling tangle!

Siri surfaced
first, looking like
a snowman. 'A
little too much
speed,' he said,
giving himself a
good shake.

'Wow!'
laughed Harry.
'That was
fantastic!'

The GOGOs
brushed
themselves down
and then tried
a bit of skating
on the frozen

lake. None of them had ice-skates, but they all enjoyed seeing how far they could slide in their boots without falling over. Then Harry cut his bin-liner into strips – enough for everyone to tie a piece over each of their boots. Soon they were spinning and skidding about like crazy and taking turns to get rides in Siri's box.

Then, just as they were at their most helpless with laughter . . . 'SNOWBALL ATTACK!' yelled Jack.

Boris and Sam were letting fly at them from up the hill!

Chapter 8

'How embarrassing,' sighed Siri when it was all over and the GOGOs were off the ice on firmer ground.

The others agreed. They hadn't landed a single snowball on Sam and Boris, who had launched their bombardment from behind the trees. By the time the GOGOs had skidded off the lake to make their own snowballs, Boris and Sam had scored direct hits on all of them and got clean away.

It was thinking about being trapped that

made Harry and his friends remember
the people stuck in their houses up at
Huntingdon. As they trudged up the slope
towards the farmhouse, Siri told them about
a letter he had read in his dad's newspaper.
It was from a man who remembered the
dreadful winter of 1947.

The writer was a boy back then. His village was cut off by snow, so he decided to take action. He collected bags of flour from his neighbours and loaded them on to his pony. Then he dragged the pony miles through deep snow to the next village and asked the baker to turn the flour into bread. When the loaves were ready, the boy loaded them on to his pony and set off home again. It was dark by the time the boy returned. Early the next morning, the neighbours were amazed and delighted to have fresh bread delivered to their doors!

'That's a great idea!' cried Jack. 'Let's pool our pocket money and buy . . . I don't know . . . some cakes or chocolate biscuits or something. And tea to drink. Old people love that sort of thing. It would really cheer them up if we arrived unexpectedly with loads of goodies.'

'Hear, hear!' said Charlie. 'But where are we going to borrow a pony from?'

'What about a car?' suggested Siri.

'Even better!' agreed Charlie. 'But who do we know with the guts to drive their car through deep snow? Would Boris help us, Harry?'

Harry wasn't sure. 'It's worth a try, I suppose,' he said doubtfully. 'He might do it to show Sam what a hero he is.'

In the kitchen at Harry's house, Boris stood with his hands on his hips and looked very important while the GOGOs

told him their plan.

'Listen, you lot,' he drawled. 'Are you
seriously asking me to deliver chocolate
biscuits to complete strangers up in
Huntingdon? You honestly want me to risk
my engine and my paintwork for that? You
must be mad! For goodness' sake, just go

away and practise dodging snowballs or something.'

Sam smirked at Harry, and dragged Boris into the living-room to drink hot chocolate and sit by the fire.

The GOGOs were disappointed, but they were not surprised – or put off. Luckily Siri had a plan. When they all went home for lunch, they secretly tucked away most of what they were given. So when they

got together again, they had quite a feast
– sandwiches, pots of yoghurt, crisps, nuts,
bananas. Siri brought piles of delicious
Kavun cakes and Jack had smuggled out
some of his mother's famous shortbread.

'This is going to be a real treat,' said
Charlie, pleased with their collection.

Off went the GOGOs, each of them
wearing a rucksack. The plan was to
struggle up the snow-bound lane to

Huntingdon on foot. But first they went over to Wedge's dad's farm to drop off the spray-gun they'd borrowed for the sculpture competition.

When they got there, a flashing violet light and a fizzing sound led them to an outbuilding where Wedge was doing his favourite thing – welding! As they approached, he tipped back the dark visor on his special helmet and gave the gang a sooty grin. 'Done it!' he beamed. 'What d'ya reckon?'

There was only one word for it: WOW! Wedge had just fitted a huge snowplough to the front of his truck.

'It was Dad's idea,' he explained. 'He wants me to clear the tracks to some of the

outlying fields so we can get food out to the sheep and cattle. Wanna jump in while I see if it works?'

The GOGOs all looked at each other. They were thinking the same thing. Siri's eyes were wide with excitement.

'Yes, please!' said Harry. 'Only, if it does work, then we might just need your help to do a little job . . .'

Chapter 9

The snow in the lane to Huntingdon
turned out to be deeper than anyone had
imagined. Wedge's snowplough worked well
and the truck's engine had plenty of power,
but it was slow-going.

Wherever the lane sank between banks
or where there were no trees to give
protection from the falling snow, deep
drifts had formed. Black smoke gathered
in clouds round the truck as the engine
growled and roared, and Wedge went at the

drifts like a battering ram.

The GOGOs did their bit; Jack and Charlie sat with Wedge and urged him on, while Siri and Harry trudged up ahead to show him the way. Sometimes, they were almost up to their necks in snow.

'Come on, you can do it!' Charlie yelled, trying to encourage the truck to shove even harder.

But in two hours they had cleared less than a quarter of the lane. Then the whole of the front section of the truck was swallowed by a great white wave of snow. The back wheels screamed as they spun. They were stuck. Again.

'Take a break!' ordered Wedge through the open window of his cab. 'We've given it

our best shot. But it looks like we're never gonna make it, guys!' He switched off the engine and pulled on the handbrake.

'We'll have to try to walk up like we planned,' said Siri, heading back towards the truck. 'But we could be in over our heads.'

Suddenly Harry had a thought that made him stand up straight. 'We need serious back-up!' he breathed to himself. 'And this is really important. I wonder . . .'

He threw down his gloves and felt in his pocket. His fingers found the key-ring. He could feel his two keys – and something else . . . something warm.

It looked like a B.U.D. was ready to help! Harry ran his finger and thumb across the smooth plastic figure on the card. *Nose-to-tail.*

WHAM!

A terrible force sent Harry sprawling sideways. He picked himself up and found himself looking at a creature of astonishing size and power. It was a cross between a three-horned rhino and a garbage truck. Its head was about one third of the size of its armoured body. Behind its head was a bony plate or frill the size of a church door.

The beast turned to look at Harry.
It lowered its head and, for a terrifying
moment, looked as though it was about to
charge. Then it opened its beak-like mouth.
'I am at your service,' it rumbled.

'T-t-triceratops?' stammered Harry.

'That is correct,' replied the creature. 'This is clearly a job for me . . .' Triceratops trotted over to the truck and hooked his biggest horn under the back of the truck, pulling it clear of the snowdrift.

'W-what's going on?' yelled Wedge. 'I've got the brake on, but we're slipping backwards!'

Triceratops unhooked himself, took a few steps back from the truck and lowered his great head. He began to paw the ground like a giant bull. Although he knew the dinosaur was invisible to everyone else, Harry was still surprised to see that he left no footprints in the snow. 'Get inside the truck – quick!' Triceratops rumbled. 'Oh, and that goes for the other small Two-Legs.'

Harry dashed round to the front of the truck. 'Quick, get in, Siri. I've, er . . . got an idea. Wedge! Let the truck roll backwards a bit more and then . . .'

'. . . give her all the power we've got?' asked Wedge.

'Right!' said Harry. The GOGOs squeezed themselves together in the warmth of the cab. As Siri closed the door

with a slam, Wedge started the engine
again.

'Hang on tight!' yelled Harry.

The roar of the engine was matched by
the grunts of Triceratops as he slammed his
nose into the smoking rear of the truck. No

one but Harry could hear the dinosaur, but they could certainly feel him.

The truck powered forward like a jumbo jet at take-off! The force of it pushed the passengers back against their seats. Powdered snow flew all around in a great white cloud and the windscreen was totally blanked out.

'I can't see a thing!' yelled Wedge. 'Brace yourselves!'

On and on went the truck. The steering wheel juddered and hopped and it was all Wedge could do to hold it steady. 'I don't get it! My foot's not touching the pedal!' he shouted.

'We seem to be gathering speed!' gasped Siri.

And then suddenly they were gliding as easily as a rubber duck through bubbles in the bath. The crash everyone expected never came. Instead, they came to a peaceful stop.

Wedge turned off the engine and wound down his window. He peered outside. 'I'm not sure how,' he muttered, 'but I think we're in Huntingdon!'

Chapter 10

The GOGOs tumbled out into the snow.
They found themselves by the war
memorial where the two main streets of
the village met at the highest point of
Huntingdon Hill. From here, there was a
magnificent view down into the valley
on the other side. A dazzling white carpet
stretched down for miles until it curved over
the next line of hills.

A large circle the size of a circus tent had
been dug out of the deep snow where the

two roads met. A group of men in big layers
of warm clothing leaned on shovels and
stared at them, open-mouthed.

'How did you get up here . . .?' began
one of them, a wiry-looking old man in a
long coat.

'The police told us they couldn't send a helicopter before tomorrow,' said another man, his round, red face drenched with sweat under his cap. 'So we thought at least we ought to clear a spot for it to land.'

'But *driving* up the lane? We thought that was impossible!' added the older man.

'You've got these kids to thank, really,' said Wedge. 'It was their idea to have a crack at it. To be honest, I never thought we'd make it through the drifts. I mean . . . my old truck has got some power, but somehow she come up that hill like a rocket!'

While Wedge was talking, Harry glanced behind the truck. He pretended he was taking a look back down the lane that the truck's snowplough had just cleared. There stood Triceratops, his great head nodding as he regained his breath. He looked so real, so solid, so magnificent that Harry found it impossible to believe that the others couldn't see him. For the first time, Harry noticed that he could see daylight through a hole in his tail. It crossed his mind that that must be

where the key-ring went when the dinosaur
was pocket-size.

He walked over to the giant beast.
'Thanks, B.U.D.,' he whispered, and ran his
hand tail-to-nose along the armour-plating.
He thought it would be like touching
the sides of a petrol-tanker or something.
Instead, it reminded him of rubbing his
hand over a bristly doormat.

As he moved his hand, the beast seemed to grin with his parrot-beak. 'Something tells me you'll be calling me up again very soon! You know where to find me,' it rumbled. Then he raised his three horns in a salute, closed his eyes and was gone. *Plasticated*. Harry patted the key-ring in his pocket.

A few people came out of their houses to see who the new arrivals were.

'Have you come to sort out the electricity?' asked one old lady with a walking stick, who was being helped along the icy footpath. 'I've got my wood-stove, see? But there's other folks up here who depend on the electricity for everything – cooking and heating and everything!'

She was talking eagerly to Wedge, since he seemed to be in charge.

'I'm afraid we can't help you with that,' said Wedge. 'Has the whole village lost power, then?'

'It's been on and off all the time since last night,' replied one of the men. 'Everybody's afraid it could be cut off altogether any minute.'

'Hmm,' pondered Siri. 'You say that the electricity is "on and off". It is my guess that ice has formed on the pylons, causing a short-circuit. Or maybe the weight of snow

is causing the wires
to touch now and
then.' He waved
his hand down
the valley, towards
the line of steel
poles that seemed
to march away like
giants through the
snow.

'Cor, you're a bit of a brain-box, young
man!' said the old lady, impressed.

'If we have much more ice or snow,'
continued Siri, 'the weight could do terrible
damage.'

As they were talking, Harry put his hands
in his pockets to keep warm. Through his

gloves he could feel something
warm on his key-ring again.
*Is Triceratops getting in touch
again so soon?* he wondered,
pulling out the plastic B.U.Ds.
Swinging by its tail and
glowing next to his keys was

a little flat apatosaurus. *Aha! Let's see what
you can do!* Harry thought.

While everyone else was busy talking,
and Jack and Charlie were sharing biscuits
around, Harry gave the plasticated dinosaur
a quick rub, nose-to-tail. At once, the little
crowd in the street were dwarfed by a full-
size prehistoric monster!

Apatosaurus was longer than four buses
parked end-to-end and, judging by its fat
tummy, at least twice as heavy. Harry's
gaze went from the tip of its enormous
drooping tail to its head that was
. . . well, just a bit bigger than
Harry! It looked odd,

stuck on the end of that *enormously* long neck. The dinosaur's neck snaked round and down to bring its head level with Harry's pale face. It was a lot bigger than it looked from a distance! The beast's jaws

opened wide to show great spoon-
shaped teeth. Vegetarian or not, this
dinosaur was scary. A hot wind hit
Harry like a hurricane, and at the
same time there came a terrible stink,
like rotting compost.

Harry was knocked flat on his
back!

Chapter 11

Harry opened his eyes to see Jack, Siri and Charlie looking down at him anxiously.

'Are you all right, Harry?' asked Charlie. 'You must have fainted or something!'

'Whoops!' thundered a voice from the strange, bug-eyed dinosaur face that hovered above his friends' heads. 'Forgive me, Harry. Indigestion. It happens when I move too fast. It's the gizzard stones in my belly. They bounce about and grind together.'

'Do me a favour!' said Harry to Apatosaurus, covering his nose.

The GOGOs were delighted to see signs of life in their friend. They thought he was talking to them, so they squatted down to get closer. It was lucky that they had no idea that the head of one of the biggest dinosaurs ever seen on earth was hovering close by.

'A favour? What do you need, Harry?' asked Charlie.

'Clear the snow and ice off those pylons,' Harry ordered Apatosaurus, pointing down the valley.

'Are you kidding?' said Jack.

'He must have banged his head,' guessed Siri.

'He needs air!' said Charlie.

'Consider it done, Harry!' rumbled

Apatosaurus. The dinosaur was a slow

mover, but he seemed to enjoy plunging

down the snowy slope towards the

nearest pylon. He floated on

his belly like a funny-

looking giant swan.

Harry pushed

himself up

on to his elbow to try to get a better look.

Wedge stepped forward. 'Up you come, mate!' he said. He put a strong arm round Harry's shoulders and hoisted him up on to his feet. Now Harry had the perfect view down the hill.

Nobody else could see anything unusual – but what they *heard* made them all jump. While everyone was fussing over Harry, dusting him down and rubbing the back of his head, there was a sudden explosion.

FSSSSSSHHH-BONGGGG!

Harry watched as Apatosaurus gave the nearest pylon a hefty swipe with his great long tail. The effect was like an earthquake.

'What was that?' Charlie yelled as everyone turned to look.

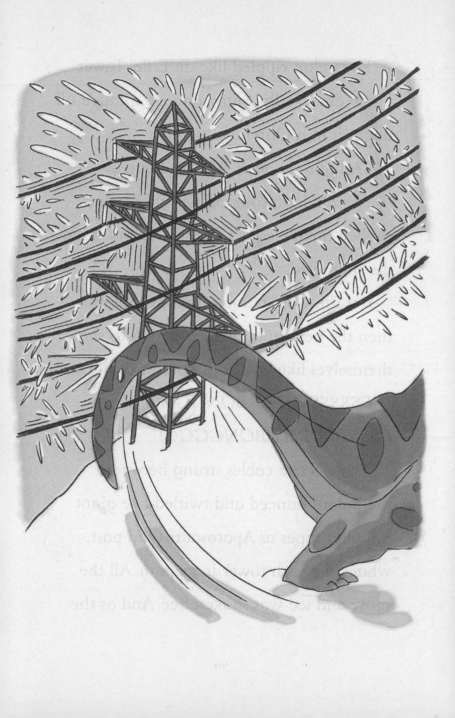

The pylon rippled like an Eiffel Tower
made out of jelly. Snow and ice sprayed all
about it in a glistening cloud.

'Did you see *that*?' Wedge shouted.

The old lady took off her glasses and
rubbed them clean. 'I must be seeing things,'
she mumbled.

But she wasn't. Soon the next pylon,
then the next and the next began to shake
themselves like wet dogs just out of the sea.

FSSSSSSHHH-BONGGGG!

FSSSSSSHHH-BONGGGG!

The electric cables strung between
the pylons danced and twirled like giant
skipping ropes as Apatosaurus slid past,
whacking each tower in its path. All the
snow and ice was shaken free. And as the

thin, white mist of snow and ice fell gently towards the ground, the sun broke out.

Before long, most of the villagers were gathered in the village hall with Wedge and the GOGOs. They were all discussing the shudders that had shaken the ice from the pylons.

'We don't get earthquakes here,' said the old lady who'd seen it, shaking her head. 'But I just can't imagine what else it could be.'

'Who cares?' said one of the other villagers. 'The power is back on!'

Everyone nodded and raised their cups of hot tea and coffee. The treats that the children had brought with them went down

very well, especially the biscuits and the homemade Sri Lankan baking.

'Deee-licious! What does your mum do? Is she a chef?' lots of admiring ladies asked Siri.

'No. She is a professor of mathematics, same as my dad,' Siri replied proudly, munching on some crisps.

'Ooh, fancy!'

Someone gave a speech about kids today being *much* nicer and more thoughtful than they said on the telly. The GOGOs pressed Harry to stand up and make a speech in reply. He did his best, but he was suddenly overcome with shyness and could only think of, 'Thank you very much. You're welcome ... It was nothing, really ...' before he sat down again.

Charlie looked at her mobile. 'Wow!' she exclaimed. 'I've got a signal. There's a text

from my mum. She says do I know where Siri is? His parents are worried because they can't get through to him and they're thinking of calling the police.'

'I wish they wouldn't worry so much!' complained Siri.

'Bad luck, Siri,' said Charlie. 'Wait. Looks like they haven't called the police after all. My mum says she's phoned Harry's mum. And Harry's mum has sent a car out looking for us.'

'Oh, no! My mum's at work,' groaned Harry. 'She must have sent Boris and Sam to collect us. That is really *embarrassing*! Can you text Sam? Tell her we're OK and that she and Boris can pick us up at the bottom of Huntingdon Lane in half an hour.'

That was pretty much the end of the celebrations. They stayed for a little while longer, but all the excitement had gone out of the GOGOs.

From heroes to zeroes in one minute flat.

Chapter 12

The kids got a nice warm send-off from the villagers as they piled into the cab of Wedge's truck. Wedge had set the plough down a notch so that he could shave off a bit more snow on the way down. 'Then they can get a gritter-lorry up here,' he called out of his window to Len, the old man in the black coat. He got a thumbs-up in reply.

'Tell you what,' said Harry. 'I fancy a go on Charlie's homemade snowboard. If it's

OK with Charlie, let me go ahead down the lane – and you can pick me up if I have any problems.'

'Go on, then,' said Charlie, who thought it might be funny to watch. 'See how you get on.'

To the cheers of the villagers, Harry managed to go five metres before he fell off. Then he slid a few more metres. Off again.

'Go on, Harry! You can do it!' yelled Jack, encouragingly. 'Lean out more!' Jack was easily the best of the GOGOs at sports, so Harry paid special attention to what he said.

It worked! Gradually, Harry got the hang of the thing and soon he had shot down the side of the lane, round the corner and out of sight.

'Apatosaurus!' he called out. 'Where are you?' Because the beast had trudged off down the hill to clear the ice, Harry hadn't been able to rub it tail-to-nose and make him plasticated again. Apatosaurus was still out there in the snow and could be up to anything by now!

He heard a shuffling noise behind him as the huge dinosaur came towards him.

'Here I am, Harry,' he said. 'What can I do for you now?'

'I'm all right, thanks,' replied Harry. 'But well done for saving the village. If the people could thank you, they would. But then they'd have to see you, and that might cause all sorts of problems!' he smiled.

'Happy to be of service,' said Apatosaurus. 'You know you can call on any dinosaur you need, any time.'

Harry looked down the lane. 'I have to get down there and meet my sister,' he said, rolling his eyes.

The dinosaur made a gentle sound, almost like a laugh. 'Hop aboard,' he said, lowering his head.

Harry didn't need to be asked twice. In a flash he was astride Apatosaurus's neck and gripping with his knees like a champion jockey. Up he rose, the dinosaur's long neck hoisting Harry way up over the trees like a fireman's ladder. What a feeling! Then the dinosaur pushed himself off on to his belly and they slid down the hill, gathering speed.

'*Wheeee!*' screamed Harry, clinging on for
dear life. 'This is better than a bob-sleigh!'

They were *hurtling* down the lane! The
rushing wind took Harry's breath away. He
was thinking that they had probably broken
the land-speed record.

They turned the corner towards the
bottom of the road, with Harry sailing up
high on the dinosaur's long neck. And that
was how Harry got a bird's-eye view of
Boris and Sam preparing *another* ambush.
They had parked Boris's sports car and
were both by the side of the road, digging
away in the drifts to make a huge pile of
snowballs. Harry could hear them cackling
with excitement as they got their ambush
ready.

'Uh-oh!' said Harry. 'Put your brakes on,
Apatosaurus.' The great beast straightened

his front legs, dug in and leaned back. By the time they had slithered to a halt, they were close enough to Harry's sister and her boyfriend to get splattered with snowballs.

Not this time, you don't! Harry thought to himself. 'Apatosaurus, quick, put me up high in that chestnut tree, the one that Sam and Boris are hiding under!'

Apatosaurus obeyed. It tilted its neck and lowered him on to a strong branch with great care. Not a snowflake fell to give him away. Then Harry whispered into the bristle-coated earhole that hovered near his mouth, 'When I say the word, give the trunk of this tree a whack with your tail.' Then he placed Charlie's snowboard in the dinosaur's mouth, and Apatosaurus lowered it gently to the ground.

'Oh, *hell-o-oo!*' sang Harry. Boris

and Sam froze and then
started looking all
around in panic.

'I'm up here,' said Harry.
'Nice try, but you won't
get us this time. And, by the
way, Boris . . . I never miss.'
Lowering his voice a little,
he added, '*Ready when you are,
B.U.D.!*'

With a stinging slap,
Apatosaurus whipped the
tree trunk hard. Harry felt

like a sailor clinging to the mast of a ship in a storm. For a second he found himself hanging upside down, but somehow he managed to scramble upright.

The sports car had disappeared completely under an avalanche of snow. As for Boris and Sam, they got buried right up to their chests.

'I think I'm going to give you a new name,' Harry confided to Apatosaurus as the dinosaur lowered him to the ground while Boris and Sam cleared snow from their faces. He paused to wave at Wedge and the rest of the GOGOs, who had just arrived in the truck. 'I think A-*WHACK*-osaurus would suit you very nicely!'

Chapter 13

'My beautiful car!' Boris was wailing.

Sam wasn't worried about that. She was furious. 'You think you're so clever!' she raged. 'I told you it was stupid to park under the trees. All my brother had to do was climb up on to a branch and set off an avalanche!'

'If only,' muttered Harry to himself and the B.U.D. 'Thanks for the help,' he whispered to Apatosaurus, then he ran his hands along the dinosaur's flanks tail-to-nose. It disappeared without a trace, back to his key-ring, waiting to be called on again.

With the B.U.D. safely plasticated, he turned his attention to helping Wedge and the GOGOs with a spot of digging. First they concentrated on freeing the spluttering Boris and Sam. Getting a tow-rope on the sports car took longer. Once the rope was secure, Wedge revved the engine of his mighty truck and slowly heaved the car out.

'Nice little motor,' said Wedge. 'No sign of any damage at all. Still, you've got a fair bit of snow packed in the vents. Probably best if I tow her along to your place, eh? Just to be on the safe side.'

Boris spluttered and growled, and looked as if he wished the snow would swallow him up again.

Later that week, Wedge's photo was in the local paper, alongside the story of his heroic rescue of a whole village.

LOCAL MAN SAVES VILLAGE

Sam was on the phone to him for hours. 'Oh, you soppy great lump,' she cooed. 'Fancy risking your life like that!'

'What about me and Charlie and Jack and Siri?' said Harry, getting annoyed. 'We were in the photo, too, you know. And it was our idea to clear Huntingdon Lane.'

Sam made a face at him. 'What's that?' she asked Wedge as she went out of the door. 'Oh, Boris? Well, you know how much I hate golf . . .' She headed somewhere private to continue their conversation.

Harry punched the air. *She's seen sense at*

last, he thought. Finally the sofa was free, the telly was available and there wasn't a golfing DVD in sight.

His phone pinged. Charlie had sent a text.

Shame! Tom Powell won best snow skulpchure. :-(

The spelling was terrible, but the message was clear – and it *was* a shame.

Just then, Harry caught sight of old Tom Powell himself wandering past the side window. He was heading down the drive towards the back of Harry's house.

Before he had time to ding on the bell, Harry opened the back door.

'Congratulations on the sculpture contest, Tom,' he said, trying to hide his disappointment.

'Thanks, Harry,' he puffed. 'But I just popped round to let you know I reckons that polar bear what your mate done was miles better than my old pirate ship,' he said quietly. 'And that igloo was pretty good, too.'

'That's really kind of you,' Harry said, smiling as best as he could.

'And another thing,' said Tom. He paused for a bit of a cough. 'My sister called from up Huntingdon. Disabled now, she is, and she's been very low. But when she spoke to me on the phone, I can honestly say she was bright as a button. Said you youngsters cheered the villagers up for days. She told me you and your mates deserve medals for what you done!'

'Oh . . . w-well . . . th-that's very . . .' stammered Harry, blushing.

'Look, I know you kids wouldn't be able to do much with a medal. So I was just wondering if you couldn't make more use of . . . this.' He  ducked round the corner of the house and reappeared pulling a fabulous-looking toboggan.

'It's a good un,' Tom assured Harry. 'Look here. The runners are steel-lined for extra speed. But it's no good to me. I want you and your mates to have it, son.'

Harry could hardly speak. 'Thanks, Tom!' he managed to say in the end. 'The GOGOs are never going to believe this!'

Of course, they were as surprised and thrilled as he had been. On their first run down through the village past the church, Harry took the driving position.

'Hey! You seem to know what you're doing,' said Jack, with admiration. 'We haven't crashed once yet!'

'You haven't been practising tobogganing with some expert we don't know about, have you?' laughed Charlie.

Harry smiled, remembering Apatosaurus speeding down the hill on his belly. *Now that would be telling!* he thought to himself.

But what he said to Charlie, Jack and Siri was ...

'*WAH-HOOOOO!*'